MONKEY
NOT READY FOR
KINDERGARTEN

Montrey: Not ready for Kindergarten
Marc Brown

DRAGONFLY BOOKS New York

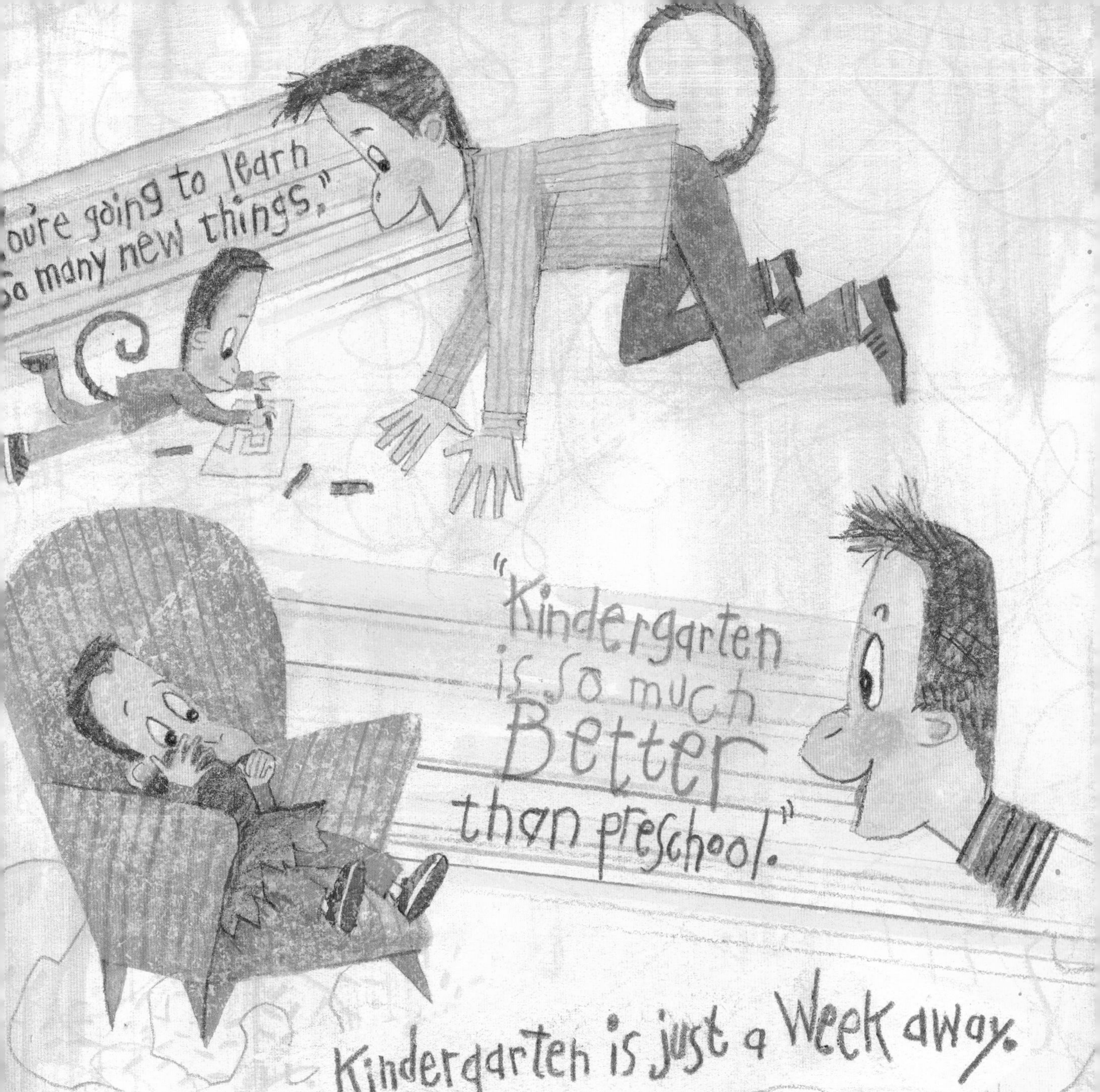

Kindergarten is just a week away.

What if his teacher doesn't like him?

What if he gets on the wrong bus?

What if he can't find the bathroom?

What if they have peas for snacks?

What if they don't have <u>red</u> crayons?

What if he can't remember the whole alphabet?

What if he doesn't make new friends?

He can already count to 12, and he usually remembers most of the alphabet.

He gets a backpack and some new sneakers with orange laces.

But he's still not ready.

Back at home,
Monkey plays school.

He lets all the
students color
with their favorite
crayons,
and he teaches them
how to count to
12.

1234
5678
91011
12

When it's his brother's turn
to be the teacher,
he tells Monkey about
show-and-tell and music class.
He teaches
Monkey
about using
Inside Voices.

At the library, Monkey and his parents read all the books about Kindergarten.

"You'll read lots of books at school."

"Probably some of your favorites."

Kindergarten doesn't sound **too** bad. But Monkey is still not ready.

"They have a special Reading Rug."

The day before Kindergarten, Monkey has a playdate with some of the kids who will be in his class.

"It's going to be so much fun!"

The night before Kindergarten, Monkey helps make his lunch.

He tucks his favorite book about bugs deep down into his backpack. Something to remind him of home.

He counts to twelve in the bathtub.

He falls asleep practicing the alphabet.

And then it's the **Big Day.**

Mommy and Daddy give Monkey hugs and kisses.

And he gives them the secret goodbye handshake they practiced.

For
·Bonnie Brown Walmsley·

All rights reserved. Published in the United States by Dragonfly Books,
an imprint of Random House Children's Books, a division of Penguin Random House LLC,
New York. Originally published in hardcover in the United States by Alfred A. Knopf,
an imprint of Random House Children's Books, New York, in 2015.

Dragonfly Books with the colophon is a registered trademark of Penguin
Random House LLC.

Visit us on the Web! randomhousekids.com

Educators and librarians, for a variety of teaching tools, visit us at
RHTeachersLibrarians.com

The Library of Congress has cataloged the hardcover edition of this work as follows:
Brown, Marc Tolon, author, illustrator.
Monkey : not ready for kindergarten / by Marc Brown. — First edition.
p. cm.
Summary: Kindergarten is just a week away and Monkey is not ready, but with help and
encouragement from family and friends, he begins to get excited.
ISBN 978-0-553-49658-1 (trade) — ISBN 978-0-553-49659-8 (lib. bdg.) —
ISBN 978-0-399-55954-9 (pbk.) — ISBN 978-0-553-49660-4 (ebook)

[1. First day of school—Fiction. 2. Kindergarten—Fiction. 3. Monkeys—Fiction.]
I. Title.
PZ7.B81618Mk 2015 [E]—dc23   2014002818

MANUFACTURED IN CHINA
10 9 8 7 6 5 4 3 2 1
First Dragonfly Books Edition
Random House Children's Books supports the First Amendment
and celebrates the right to read.